A Doll for Navidades

by ESMERALDA SANTIAGO

Illustrated by ENRIQUE O. SÁNCHEZ

SCHOLASTIC PRESS • NEW YORK

This story is an adaptation of Esmeralda Santiago's essay "A Baby Doll Like My Cousin Jenny's,"
which originally appeared in the December 1996 issue of *Sí* magazine.

LIBRARY OF CONGRESS CATALOGING-IN-PUBLICATION DATA

Santiago, Esmeralda. · A doll for Navidades / by Esmeralda Santiago ; illustrated by Enrique O. Sánchez.— 1st ed.   p. cm.
Summary: While preparing for Christmas in Puerto Rico, seven-year-old Esmeralda asks the Three Magi for a baby doll like
her cousin's, but when they bring something else instead she gains a deeper understanding of the meaning of the holiday.
ISBN 0-439-55398-9 (alk. paper)
[1. Christmas—Puerto Rico—Fiction. 2. Dolls—Fiction. 3. Gifts—Fiction. 4. Family life—Puerto Rico—Fiction. 5. Puerto Rico—Fiction.]
I. Sánchez, Enrique O., 1942-, ill. II. Title. PZ7.S23823Bab 2005   [E]—dc22 2004019193

10 9 8 7 6 5 4 3 2 1   05 06 07 08 09
Printed in Singapore   46   First edition, October 2005
Text set in Edwardian Medium. The display type was set in Bellevue. The illustrations were rendered in acrylic on canvas.
Book design by Marijka Kostiw

To Delsa and to Papi — E. S.

To my cousins Tutin, Hugo, Salvador, Maximo, and

Freddy Beras-Goico — E. O. S.

I was seven and had never had a doll.
I wanted a baby doll like my cousin Jenny's, with pink
skin and blue eyes that shut when she lay her down.

Jenny's doll was the size of a small baby, its chubby arms and legs slightly bent, its tiny fingers open to reveal a hand with deep furrows and mounds.

Las Navidades were coming. Our neighbors hung crocheted snowflakes along the eaves of their tin roofs and set out flaming-red poinsettias on their porches. My sisters and brother and I helped Papi tie crepe paper around the hibiscus and gardenia bushes. We also helped Mami pick oregano leaves and dry, crackly *achiote* pods with powdery red seeds inside.

In school, we sang about *Nochebuena*, the night Baby Jesus was born, and about *Los Tres Reyes Magos*, who were following a bright star to Bethlehem on their camels. The night before *El Día de los Tres Reyes Magos*, we would leave water and grass for the camels, and in the morning, we would wake to find presents that the Three Magi had brought to our houses after traveling thousands of miles.

The smells of Christmas floated from Mami's kitchen: ginger and cloves, cinnamon and coconut, oregano, rosemary, garlic.

Thick, gray smoke curled from other yards where pigs roasted, their skin crackling and sizzling to the strumming of *cuatros*, the scratching of *güiros*, the *aguinaldos* about *Nochebuena* and about the Three Magi.

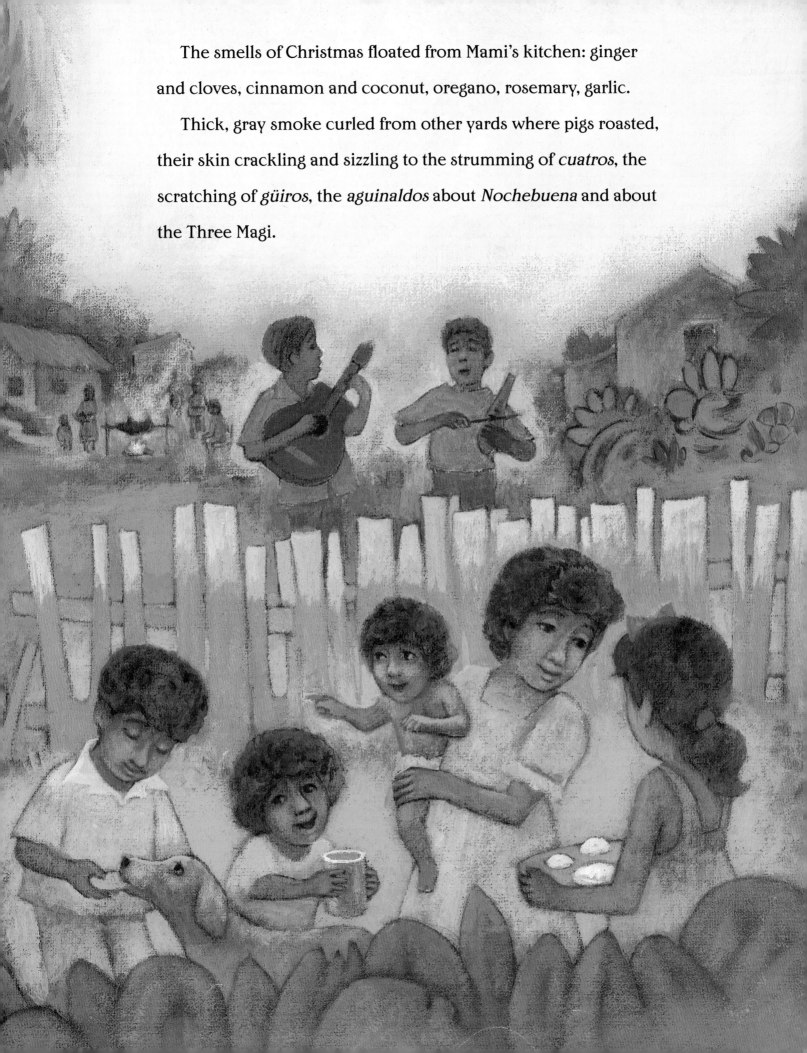

At night, *parrandas* surprised their sleeping neighbors with songs. The *parrandas* went from house to house, playing music and singing *aguinaldos* in exchange for a piece of roasted pork, or a *pastel* wrapped in a banana leaf, or slices of guava paste pressed on chunks of white cheese.

On *Nochebuena*, we went to the *Misa de Gallo*. We walked to church holding candles because the mass began at midnight. It was so dark that all we could see were the eyes of night creatures in the bushes beyond the trembling circles of candlelight.

Even though we tried not to, we sometimes fell asleep during the *Misa de Gallo*, because it went on for a long time. Mami and Papi had to carry us home, asleep on their shoulders, as the roosters were beginning to sing to the rising sun of Christmas morning.

When we woke up on Christmas Day, Mami and Papi gave us cloth pouches filled with walnuts, hazelnuts, and almonds in their shells. Papi showed us how to crack the shell with a rock so that we could get the delicious meat inside.

Mami made *arroz con dulce*, which tasted sweet and coconutty and had sticks of cinnamon that we sucked on for a long time.

A week after *Nochebuena*, we celebrated the New Year with noisemakers and more singing and dancing, and we were happy because Three Kings' Day was coming.

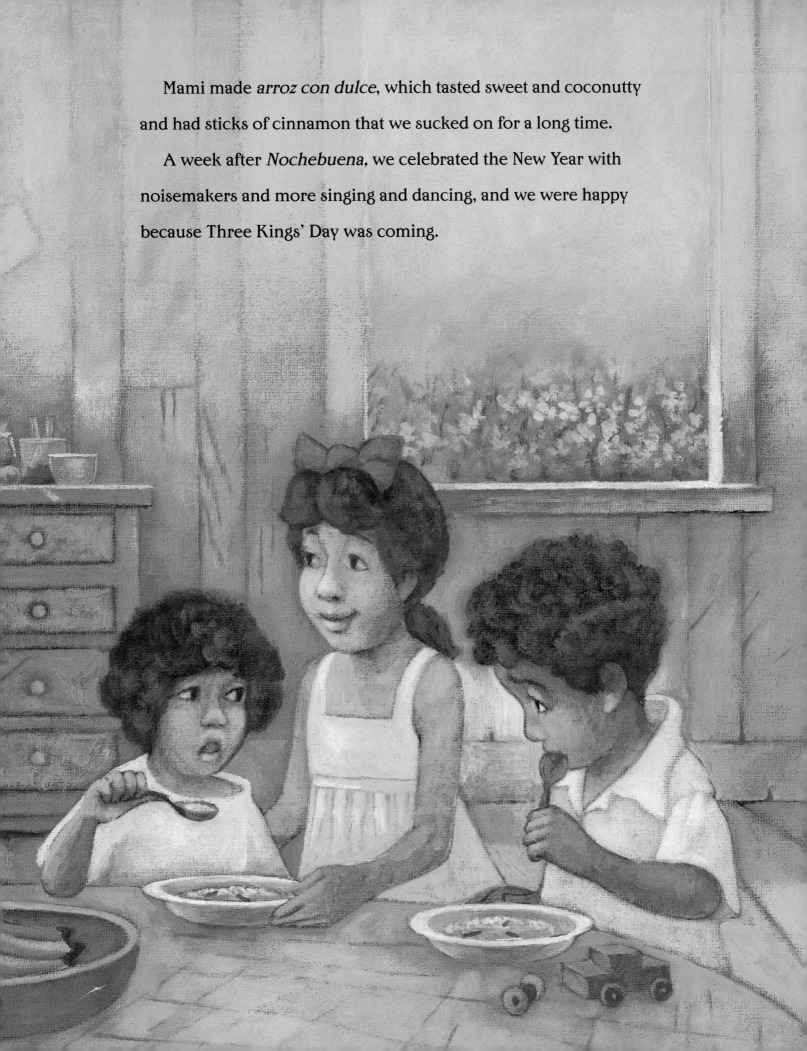

I wrote a letter to the Three Magi on Papi's special paper.

He let me borrow his pen, too, so I couldn't make mistakes

because the ink could not be erased.

Dear Three Magi :
I have been good this year,
you can ask Mami and Papi
if you don't believe me.
I would like a baby doll
like my cousin Jenny's
with blue eyes that close.

I hope you like the water
I left and the grass for
the camels.
Have a good journey.
Sincerely,

Esmeralda Santiago

Delsa, who was five, asked me to write a note for her, too.

"Ask the Three Magi," she said, "for a baby doll like the

one Jenny has."

"But that's what I want!" I said.

"We can both get one, and they can be sisters," she said.

I didn't want her to have a doll like mine, so for Delsa, I wrote:

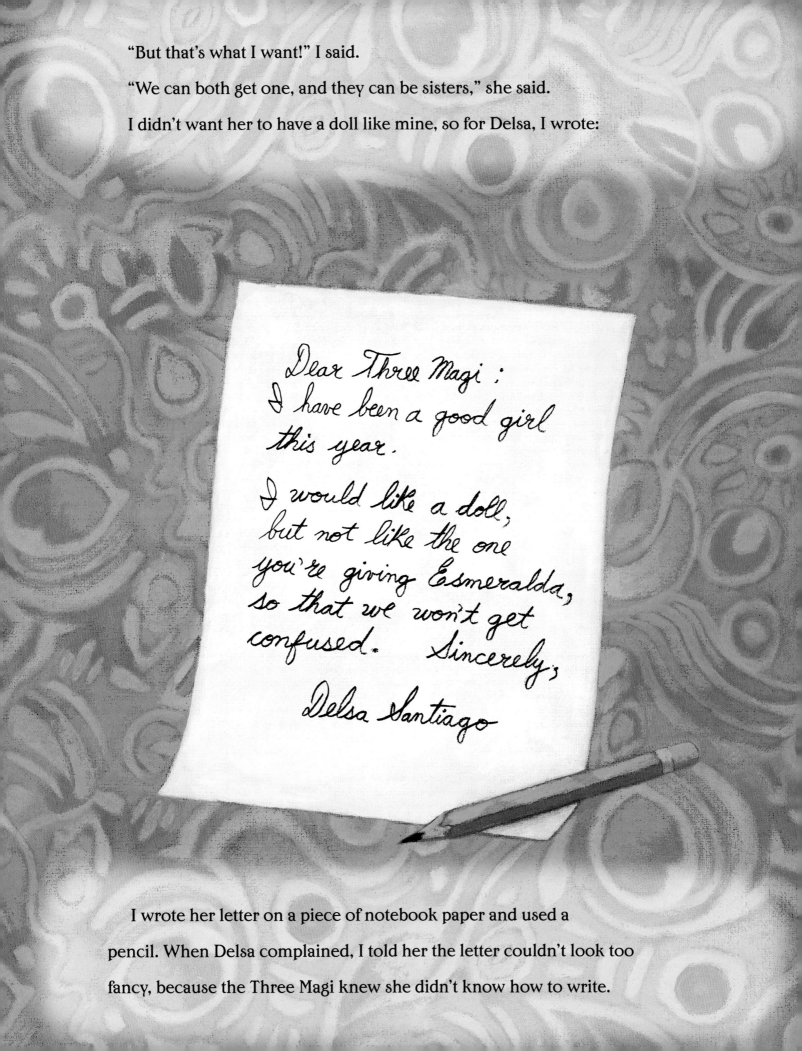

Dear Three Magi :
I have been a good girl
this year.

I would like a doll,
but not like the one
you're giving Esmeralda,
so that we won't get
confused.   Sincerely,
Delsa Santiago

    I wrote her letter on a piece of notebook paper and used a
pencil. When Delsa complained, I told her the letter couldn't look too
fancy, because the Three Magi knew she didn't know how to write.

The night before the Three Magi came, my sisters and brother and I

searched the yard for tender blades of grass to leave inside our shoes for

the Magi's camels. We put the shoes under our beds, the toes sticking

out so that the Magi would see them, with my note inside my shoes and

Delsa's inside hers. Next to the shoes we left cans of water.

The other kids grumbled that it wasn't fair that we wrote

to the Magi and they didn't. But Mami told them that the Magi

would bring gifts even without a letter.

I woke up while it was still dark. Two shadows moved around the room, carrying bundles in their hands. I closed my eyes quickly. It must be two of the Magi, I thought, while the third stays outside with the camels.

Next time I opened my eyes, it was daylight and Delsa was squealing in my ear. "Look, look! I got a baby doll just like Jenny's!"

I scrambled out of bed, looked under it, and found a flat, rectangular package under my shoes. It didn't look big enough to hold a baby doll.

Inside was a board game of a racetrack with horses running around it.

Papi saw my disappointment and asked, "Don't you like it?" Mami looked at me with a worried expression.

"I wanted a doll," I cried, "like that one!" I grabbed the doll from Delsa's arms. She grabbed it back and ran to the porch.

Mami and Papi looked at each other. Mami knelt and hugged me. "You're a big girl, this game is for a big girl."

"But I asked for a doll," I sobbed.

Papi took my hand and walked me to the yard.

"I'm sorry, *mi'ja*," Papi said. "It looks like by the time the Three Magi came to our house, they had only one doll left. They know you are a big girl. You will understand better than Delsa."

"It's not right!" I cried. "The Three Kings are magic. Why can't they make enough baby dolls for everybody?"

Papi looked at me, his face as sad as I felt. He looked so unhappy that I knew he was disappointed, too.

"Maybe next year," he said. "I hope so."

"*Sí*, maybe next year." I hugged him, and kissed his smooth cheek.

I went over to Delsa. She pressed the doll tightly to her chest.

"Can I see it?" I said.

She handed it to me, but kept her fingers wrapped around the doll's arm.

I loved the way it smelled, rubbery sweet.

"Did you give her a name yet?" I asked.

"Rosita," she said. "You can be her godmother if you want."

"*¡Ay, sí!* I'd like that!"

"Give her back now," Delsa said.

I was seven, and had never had a doll. But being a *madrina* to Rosita was almost as good.

A *colibrí* fluttered around a hibiscus flower. It floated over the red petals, its wings humming. I watched it go from flower to flower, hovering briefly over each, then flying on to the next one.

The *colibrí* was like the Three Magi going from house to house leaving presents for children. It was like Mami and Papi when they kissed me, my sisters, and brother good night, telling each of us, "I love you."

The hummingbird flew away until it was a speck against the turquoise sky, but I knew that, like the Magi, it would be back.

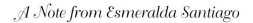

A Note from Esmeralda Santiago

I am the eldest in a family of eleven children, and I spent most of my childhood in Puerto Rico. *A Doll for Navidades* is based on what happened on my seventh *Día de los Tres Reyes Magos*, although some details have been changed for this picture book. My sister Delsa still remembers the story and says that I was a good godmother to Rosita. While this is my first book for children, I have written several books about my life for adults, including *When I Was Puerto Rican*, *Almost a Woman*, and *The Turkish Lover*. I live in Westchester County, New York, with my husband and two children.

A Note from Enrique O. Sánchez

I grew up in the Dominican Republic, on an island just west of Puerto Rico. My family celebrated *las Navidades* with many of the same traditions that Esmeralda describes. I excitedly set out shoes with grass and water by my bed, but to make sure I got more gifts from the Magi, I also left a shoe at my grandparents' house next door and another at my uncle's house nearby! I am primarily a fine arts painter, and I have also enjoyed illustrating thirteen other picture books for children. I live in northeastern Vermont with my wife and often visit our artist son in New York City.

Glossary of Spanish Words
NOTE THAT IN SPANISH, THE "R" SOUND IS ROLLED, AS IN A PURR

achiote: [ah-chee-oh'-teh] herb plant; the red powder inside the dried seeds is used for coloring and flavor

aguinaldo: [ah-ghee-nal'-do] Christmas carol

arroz con dulce: [ah'-ros con dool'-seh] dessert made with rice and coconut milk

¡Ay, sí!: [eye, see] Oh, yes!

colibrí: [coh-lee-bree'] hummingbird

cuatro: [kwah'-tro] a ten-string guitar-like instrument

El Día de los Tres Reyes Magos: [el dee'-ah deh los tress reh'-yes mah'-gos] Three Kings' Day, celebrated January 6th

güiro: [gwee'-roh] ribbed gourd instrument

madrina: [mah-dree'-nah] godmother

mi'ja: [mee'-hah] my child

Misa de Gallo: [mee'-sah deh gah'-yo] Christmas Eve church service

las Navidades: [las nav-ee-dah'-des] Christmastime

Nochebuena: [no-cheh-bwen'-ah] Christmas Eve

parranda: [pah-rand'-dah] a group of carolers

pastel: [pas-tell'] meat-filled pastry wrapped in a folded banana leaf

los Tres Reyes Magos: [los tress reh'-yes mah'-gos] The Three Magi, also known as The Three Wise Men